Rush

Of

Many

Waters

Also by Pauly Hart

Rush of Many Waters:

Volume Nine

By Pauly Hart

ISBN: 978-1-955399-13-5
Library of Congress Catalog Data is available at: Loc.gov
This book is available at cost on Amazon.com and wherever
fine books are sold.
Any references to historical events, real people, or real
places are used fictitiously. Names, characters, and
places are products of the author's imagination.
Front Cover Art by Franz Marc:
Front cover design by Pauly Hart
Paperback version printed in Savannah, Georgia, USA,
where available.
First Edition, 2021
Author Contact: EmpiresAndGenerals@gmail.com
Author Website: PaulyHart.com

Contents

The Nibblers

"The Supreme Nibbler Conservatory of Wellston Park Limited" was printed on the outside of the box in very fancy cursive letters and it was addressed to my daughter. "To the most noteworthy of children, Brixallyn Maeve Charlington, on this, the tenth anniversary of her birth." The box was massive. Cream colored plasticine glued and sealed around the actual outer lining of the box inside.

Setting it all up was pretty easy, for inside of the large box was a clear box and instructions on which end was down. In large font, it simply said: "Place on floor, in a clear area, prominently displayed, where it will remain undisturbed for the rest of your life."

That was alarming. We had just moved into our new home. Only just - last week, that is. It was a very strange and awkward gift. We only had one child and she was a miracle. She wasn't even really ours, to tell the truth. She had been laid on our doorstep with a note: "Please take care of me." The note said, so we did, no questions.

My wife Cheryl and I had always wanted children. The doctors had told us that there was no way this could ever be achieved, but we prayed every day for it. And, one rainy night there was a knock on the door and there she was. That was ten years ago today.

It took all of my strength and that of Gallifrey, our slave, to move the box into the house. Gallifrey was a Gray man, but that was alright, it wasn't like they were actually men or anything. Gallifrey helped me install it as well. To give him credit, it was his eye that found the perfect spot in the dining room for the box. Grays were skilled at some things and not with others. Gallifrey was good with spaces and problems. He was the one who supervised the movers to get us here.

It was up, one-two-three and done. The box we put up against the wall and hit the "GO" button that was illuminated there on the front in bright blue. The entire box wobbled, measured, shot out lasers and then raised itself up on skinny legs about seven feet above the ground, right to where an adult could easily reach it, but not bump your head. There was a loud thumping as it tested the walls, found the anchors, and installed itself. It beeped politely and the blue "GO" went dead. The lasers shut off, the legs retracted, and there was a *FOOSH* as the lightweight box popped off and fell to the floor. Where there was once a kerfuffle of noise, now there was the silence of furniture. An antique wall unit, part cupboard, part curio.

Gallifrey scooped up what remained of the lightweight outer packaging and took it away to be folded into our compactor, leaving me to stare at the new installation. It was something akin to an enclosed floating wall shelf. If I were to have to guess at the design, I would have to say that Nineteenth Century French Woodworkers hand carved it all, but I would most probably be mistaken. It was a hanging shelf console of curious design, for it did not have any of the ugly brackets that usually stick out of the bottom of wall shelves, but rather they were on top, as book ends, in the shape of towers. It was very beautiful woodwork, and there was not an imperfection to be seen. It was jet black.

Just then, a tiny panel near the top middle flipped open and I half expected a coo-coo to pop out and tell me the time. Instead however, a horizontal laser scanned the room, then a vertical one. It beeped a long tone and popped and the panel closed. Then the color began to change. Growing lighter, it became a deep reddish-brown and then lighter even still. Slowly it lit itself until it resembled a mid-range sandy ivory, which complimented the room marvelously. The recesses in the inlaid carved patterns were a touch darker to give it a shabby chic appeal. It was quite beautiful and it matched the carpet, walls and all the other furniture.

Quite precisely then, my wife arrived home. The transponder dinged and its door slid open. She was clad in shopping clothes and walked in, said hello and started charging the groceries into the modpod.

"Need a hand?" I offered.

"No thanks doll, I'll just have Gallifrey unload it. Where is he?"

"He's out back," I said. "Come take a look at this would you?"

She came out from the kitchen and took a look at the box. "Oh!" She exclaimed, "what is it?"

I handed her the pamphlet that came with the box. "I have no idea but I installed it and there it is." I told her.

She read the manual, including the welcome letter that came with it, which I had not seen.

"It says that she is the proud new owner of a Nibbler, one out of a set of ten will be with her for every ten years until she is one hundred and ten years old and that she will never lack for comfort or ever be sick or ever be impoverished. That she will be part of an elite club of young people whom she will meet tomorrow and that is that." She put the letter back on the table slowly, hands shaking. There was a long pause.

I blubbered out finally: "That's fucking brilliant!" and hugged her.

Still speechless she muttered out the words: "One hundred and ten?"

Our eyes met. "One hundred and ten?" we said together and both started laughing.

Brixie arrived home from school an hour later. Still supported by the bus service, she was on a route that dropped her off right at the front door. We had been so excited about her gift that we had promptly forgotten the cake or the other presents that we had gotten her. Our dining room set off to one side, and that was where the big event was to take place. We had been in the living room, now seated on chairs, looking up at the wall unit and talking. Gallifrey had been in and out, I supposed he was going about his daily routine… Until the front door slid open and she walked in.

The little girl that lived in our hearts as our princess and our daughter had arrived. As usual, she plopped her book-bag on the couch, and walked into the kitchen, opened the fridge and said: "I'm hungry."

We were seated on kitchen chairs. Our expressions were priceless. We had not gotten ready and now all was ruined. It had been a surprise party, after all. She was not a big people person and so we had only invited Glenda, her best friend, who was to arrive very...

The doorbell rang. With panicked looks to one another, we shot up out of our chairs.

"You get the door and I'll..." my wife pointed towards the den.

"Alright. I'll stall everyone."

"Ten minutes?" Cheryl asked.

"That's pushing it. Five?" I responded.

"Done." she said and I headed toward the door.

Brixie was already at the front door, and gabbing away with them, curious as to why Glenda was there with her mother and why Glenda was trying to give her a present.

"For your party." She exclaimed. And I had a lot of explaining to do suddenly. Brixie wasn't having any of it.

"I told you Da, I wanted to not have a party." Her arms stretched out in disgust. I wanted this to be a specia..."

But her words never finished, for at that time, a most majestic tone of trumpet and organ sounds filled the room. The wall unit had begun to play music, then a melodic and booming voice followed directly after.

"Be it known that the most honorable Brixallyn Maeve Charlington has hereby today received from The Supreme Nibbler Conservatory of

Wellston Park Limited, the most coveted of all gifts that a little girl may receive, her first Nibbler." The voice was still and the music stopped. Then there was a little *hiss* and the panel on the farthest left of the box slid upward and was silent.

My wife, Cheryl took my hand. She had come in from the dining area. She gave it a little squeeze. No one moved. Glenda's mother, breaking the silence uttered a "Well?" To which I responded: "I don't know."

And then it came out. Soft green eyes and squeaked like a toy. It wasn't white, it wasn't brown, or black, or even gray. It was all of those colors with a dash of red and it looked like a chinchilla, a ferret and a sugar glider had some sort of contest to see who could make the weirdest offspring. It didn't look like anything I'd ever seen before but it was cuter than any of them.

"*Meep?*" it called and climbed and danced to the top of the top of the cabinet it had come out of and *meeped* again. Brixie immediately went up to it and it hopped into her hand. And then it disappeared. Literally disappeared. Ceased to be seen. Gone. Vanished.

And then suddenly, it was back. Not even a shimmer or a special effect. No sounds or flickering lights. Not even a tremor in the house. Just one second, not there, and one second back. She looked up at me with a sadness in her eyes, and held out her new pet. It was dead.

My wife fainted.

2

Glenda and her entire family had moved away very soon after. Still to this day we can't find out where they went or where they are. We don't know how they changed their name or how they relocated so completely, but even the school has no record now of Glenda ever attending there and the people who live at their house refuse to talk to me. At first my wife and I tried to get Brixie to talk to us about what had happened, but she couldn't seem to remember. She says that she remembers coming home from school and then waking up the next day, but nothing in between. We tried everything that we could think of. Counsellors and doctors told us that nothing was wrong with her and that everything would be alright if we just established a "normal life" for her. Whatever that meant.

In the meanwhile, we received the news that she had been accepted into a "Magnet School" for Chemical Volcanology and that we needed to act on the offer quickly. The school was out in the countryside and it was top rated. So top rated that I had never even heard of it. Heppler Winkley was a school of only two hundred. "Training and educating the brightest and most talented children in the land" was their credo and they meant business.

She was gone almost every day of the year at school. She got to come home four days a year, and these were at her disposal. We could not visit her at school, as parents were not allowed on school grounds, so we waited for her to come to us. She chose only to use one of those days each year. Her birthday.

And every birthday was the same. We sat around waiting for the box to sing to her. We gather around the cabinet to see if anything will happen. Every birthday nothing happened and she asks to be driven back to school.

She accepted the teacher's aid position at school and stayed past graduation until she was twenty. The day of her birthday, around five in the morning our doorbell rang, and it was her with all of her belongings.

"I'm hungry," she said, and went to the fridge.

Just then a most majestic tone of trumpet and organ sounds filled the room. The box had begun to play music, and then a voice followed directly after.

"Be it known that the most honorable Brixallyn Maeve Charlington has hereby today received from The Supreme Nibbler Conservatory of Wellston Park Limited, the most coveted of all gifts that a young woman may receive, her second Nibbler." The voice was still and the music stopped. Then there was a little *hiss* and the second panel from the left end of the box slid upward and was silent.

We all waited for what would happen next.

June

"There was a day in late June that I had been standing at the taxi stand in the rain thinking about her. She had left the morning earlier. I had the arduous task of sorting through her jewelry. I was trying to determine what was mine and what she had borrowed off Crysta. The task had proved more fun than I could have ever imagined. There had only been a couple of earrings to return to Crysta. Of course, nothing matched. Oh, and I guess there was that whole thing about keeping the leftovers for herself."

"I had always been quite fond of her. She had that wild sort of personality that could never be tamed, even when faced with the dire consequences of her own crazy actions. June had lived in my apartment complex for a couple of years before I had moved in. It was her birthday when we first met. She had burst out of the elevator with a load of Chinese food and spilled it all over me. Chow Mein in the hair, dirty rice down the blouse."

"She was mortified and demanded that she take care of me at once. She had been going to take the food out to the park and eat alone; something she did every year on her birthday. It had only taken a moment in her apartment and we had immediately become friends. I nixed her idea and took her out for sushi and drinks instead."

"We were neighbors, we shared common interests, but we might as well have been sisters. I had gotten her a job in the travel agency where I was working, as sort of a "temp" thing. She ran errands for the other agents and myself. Though not always having a heavy workload, she managed to keep herself occupied. The agency liked her well enough and eventually took her on full time."

"She had been my one ray of sunshine in my life when Charles (my fiancé' at the time), had left me without explanation. I cried enough to water a small garden. June had been there, tissues at the ready. We had both taken off work that Friday and rented a hotel room on the east side of town, we watched old movies and ate pizza until the sun came up that next day. I would not have known what to do without my June. She saved me from the torment of going through that alone."

"She moved in a couple of months later and our lives were transformed. We painted the walls hot pink and brown. We covered the ceiling with glow-in-the-dark stars we got at the dollar store, and began a stuffed dinosaur collection. Our friends hate it but we don't care."

"We never talked about the past. Every time I tried to talk about Charles, or even what it was like growing up the way I did, she would shut me down and demand that we do something fun. Likewise, she never talked about her past either. I respected it and we stayed happy."

"Five years ago on the anniversary of our meeting, she learned that she had AIDS. Now it was my turn to be there for her. And I was. I sat with her during every doctor's visit... and when things turned from bad to worse, I went with her to plan out her funeral. We picked out everything together and I ended up paying for most of it. She didn't have anyone. Only me."

"Now, as I stand her thinking about her, standing here in the rain, I wonder why she was taken. She was so near and dear to me. It didn't seem fair. To have a friend suddenly come into your life and then suddenly ripped from it didn't feel like the universe was doing me any favors."

"But she left us. And all I have now is her smile."

"It was the day after the funeral when I got the letter from her attorney about her will. I was floored, as I did not think that she had anything to give except her clothes, a couple of lava lamps and the stuffed dino collection. I was wrong. She had left me everything."

"I never understood why she had led the life that she had lived. Quiet and lonely, she had been so rich. She could have afforded the best treatments. She could have done so much for herself with her fortune. Her lawyer told me that the 'Frugality Disorder' she had was a type of obsessive compulsive personality disorder that was well known, but not treatable. She had been treated time and time again, only to run away with each 'success' and start a new life in another city, choosing poverty each time."

"She had everything that she had ever needed in life, if she had only reached out to take it. She was the sole inheritor to Nerata Chemical Holdings - A multimillion dollar genetics lab and research company that specialized in corn oils for the fuel industry."

Nothing could be heard except for the slight buzzing of the sound system. A glass with melting ice clinked at the front table in front of me as it melted in the crystal ware. A puddle of condensation forming on the table cloth. The dessert was untouched. Even the banquet staff did not dare move. I shuffled my notes to the last page. Every eye was riveted on me.

"Much has gone on in NCH since I came into leadership one year ago today. Our company is stronger now than it has been since June's grandfather first began work in his basement so long ago. We have seen success in the fuel industry as well as in five distinct medical research fields. Our new future in total pharmacology dedication seems to be not only a profitable path but a predestined one as well. With your help and financial support, we are launching this company wide IPO straight into the cure for our dear late friend and my personal muse and friend."

"The cure for AIDS will not be an easy road to travel. Few take this path for the fear that there is no profit in end. We walk a hamster wheel in the cycle of life, going and going but not going anywhere. We watch as others seem to make progress on the wheel and think to ourselves when we get a chance on the wheel things will be different. We live the life of 'If only' or 'someday'... The time has come to break the wheel and use it as a ladder to free us from the cage we have trapped ourselves in. But for the sake of our friends and family we must succeed. We must and we will… Find a cure for this dreadful disease."

And, as I left the stage to thunderous applause I swore I could see June there, looking up at me in all the faces of the men and women who would join me in my fight.

Hunt

>>>Accessing System Registry<<<
>>>Scanning<<<

>>>...<<<

>>Seeking<<
>>Scanning<<
>>Searching<<
>>Finding <<

>>>>>>Target Located: Renegade New Boston Biogen Lab Experiment X02-101<<<<<<<

>>Name: Aptrix Viil<<
>>Height: 5'11<<
>>Weight: 190 LBS<<
>>Race: Kimph /// Fox-Human Mutant Breed<<
>>Physical Description: Evolved fox based with human genes and cellular structure.<<
>>Status: Escaped recently from New Boston Biogen: 115 HORs ago. Kill on target.<<
>>Caution: Target is equipped with An unknown amount of Flash Thermal Energy Disruptor Pods. AKA: TED<<
>>Caution: One Flash 89.S0 disruptor pistol also in possession, fully charged.<<

The metal claws scratched the floor as they walked slowly farther down into the alley. A scruff ran passed on the floor which was immediately scanned by its registry. A light hum was heard then. It took form. Another scruff appeared on the skanky concrete floor. The new scruff silently crept along the walls and proceeded down to where the fire was burning. beckoning it to come nearer.

The renegade Kimph was sitting on a box, in front a converted barrel which was now burning hot with orange heat. Aptrix Viil was busily chewing Samone with a hint of ginseng. The scruff scurried along the wall and leapt onto the floor beside Aptrix. The fox man's ears perked up and he turned to his side, seeing the little pink critter. "Get out of here you pest!" he said, waving his gun at the little rodent. The scruff didn't move but it seemed to flicker out of distortion like an older TV set. Aptrix rubbed his eyes... Then quickly came upon the realization of what it was before him. His hands were trembling as he uttered the words in a dry whisper: "Lo-Ami".

Aptrix sprung into the air and back flipped away from the dissolving scruff, and while still in midair he shot repeatedly at the rodent. All his shots were in vain, missing just inches to the left. Another hum... Lo-Ami took form: Metal claws glinting in the fire's light. Aptrix dashed away from Lo-Ami and ran down the alleyway, back into the street. Pound. Pound. Pound. His feet and heart were speeding along quite nicely now. Lo-Ami's Plasma Quad Sequencer was locked onto Aptrix's DNA, and he rocketed down and around on Aptrix's tail almost as quickly, with the whine of his rocket booster lifting him high into the sky. The Blades on his forearms, serrated with technological keenness, began to rotate in a berserker frenzy. Aptrix, dodging left and right down the alley had to do something. Taking out a TED, he tossed it behind him in the general direction of where the killer robot might be in the next few seconds. He broke out of the darkness into the bright street, filled with dozens of glowing screens from nearby stores and nightclubs. Citizens of the city were crowded near the alleyway, as they tried to get into the Neo Sushi, one of the hottest spots in the vicinity. Aptrix made his way into the crowd of the lineup, as he quietly looked at the detonator in his hand and hit the switch.

There was no sound. No explosion. No mechanical crumpling that would have foretold of his success. Aptrix was worried. The TED had enough power to take out any mechanized menace that might try to take him out. Yet this was Lo-Ami. What had happened to him? Aptrix felt suddenly sick in the stomach, as if someone had kicked him... Lo-Ami had known about the TED Pod... and had somehow jammed it before he had a chance to detonate it. Suddenly all of the screens on the stores and even the one on the storefront of the Neo Sushi flickered and was replaced with another image, with a text banner above it:

"The capture of Aptrix Viil... Public Enemy #4576! Brought to you by Lo-Ami and Gordos Pasta Bites!" Live and in color.

All of the people in the crowd looked to him as he backed away. Seeing himself on the screen was a disorienting thing. Almost dreamlike. But where was the camera? Whirling he found it. Behind him, hovering like a guillotine was Lo-Ami. Plasma Quad at the ready. "Target Achieved" whirred the debacle. "Destroy Target". There was a great yell as all the people in the streets ducked for cover. Aptrix took cover in the crowd but Lo-Ami hovered above the Neo Sushi, and let two thick beams of blue plasma emit from the guns engulfing the whole crowd in front of the sushi bar. A huge explosion... then... nothing. No line of people. No renegade mutant. The entrance to Neo Sushi was now opened to all those waiting. But there was no one waiting. Neo Sushi's front was nothing but a big hole in the wall filled with flames and fallen steel beams... Some metal and some bone. Remnants of the crowd now gone...

COMPLETION STATUS?

>>>Mission Accomplished<<<
>>>Target Exterminated<<<
>>>Civilian Casualties<<<
>>>Scanning<<<
>>>39...<<<
>>>Scanning<<<
>>>46...<<<
>>>Scanning<<<
>>>59...<<<

IGNORE

>>>Confirmed<<<
>>>Civilian Casualties<<<
>>>0<<<

CONFIRMED

Lo-Ami burst off into the afternoon sky, with the smoke still blowing in the wind.

Poems

I want and wish

I want to share
my life with the ruler
of saints
the creator of creation
the lily of the valley
the true blue diamond
who cuts away my soul
Jesus, Jeshua, Emmanuel
King of all bosses
Saint of all Saints
Embodiment of perfection
and Lord of the Living
And ruler of the dead.

I wish to baptize
my repugnant soul
within his merciful gaze
and let him
vanquish my fears
in his river of longevity
and thought-love.

I want to progress
to the state of joy
beyond all
human complaint
to never tire
of praising him
within the scope
of his love and passion.

King of glory and
Lord of Angels
Resolve my tired
and weary soul

and redeem me.

                                                    Wichita

                    Across these newly whited plains
                         I see a distant hawk
                    The feather falls from its plume
                              like a tear
                         the harvest is plentiful
                        I hear the pasture lands
                    And Rich is in the background
                       with his hammered dulcimer
                         Lines of energy stretch
                         where trees should stand
                         and barbed wire hems in
                        the beauty of the stampede
                   for church-goers and party-throwers
                            they are the same
                      joy falls from their lips like rain

                         Red Haired Wonder

                       I've come to you my friend
                   Dealing with life is such uncertainty
                         You are my nearest love
                    A vacuum of inner despondency
                        I want to know your soul
                   Your wire frame is just not on my mind
                         The life behind your eyes
                  Betrays the pursed-lipped smile on your face.

You are a drifter girl.
A wind rider with broken reigns.

A horse in a thunder storm.
Lightning and sea-foam

drip from your hooves.

Lover of love

You are the sweetness in the murkiness of my day.
Your smile is a light to my dreary way.
The light from your eyes gives power to my step,
and your energy brings up from my soul... life, like water.
I love you my dear. You. Like no other. My best friend,
my true heart, desire so pure, thoughts so warm,
melting is my mind when it dwells upon the furnace of your ardent desire.
deep. so deep is your love. Leviathan deep is your love.
And my love so wide. Cosmonaut wide. Our loves blend,
twist and swirl into a rainbow of faces and smiles and
happy-dancy feet.
we mesh, we mold. come together and hand-in-glove fit.
We are one, we have won, we, one won.
How I long to lace and weave myself into the fabric of your inner want.
The chakra of your karma comes to me.
I grow and learn inside your mind and know, always learning.
I know your mind, your soul together spun with mine, forever twine.

Waltz in the park

I think that it was November
when the leaves were changing
and I was climbing the trees they

belonged to
When I had fun with nature
in the autumnal equinox time
and life was just a fun time
   with my girlfriend
You might think that we were
nuts or a little loony
running nature trails together
   bare-footed then
But looking into our eyes
You could see God and charity
And total abandonment to life
   all for God
Was it in November, or now
I seem to remember feeling this
It was yesterday and it was
   right here

horace the significant

i am not a winner, nor shall i ever be
i am not a survivor, and do not pretend
i am a coward and a loser, and care not at all
i am nothing, hear nothing, and become less

i do not matter, i am forgotten, and alone
i do nothing right, and my trials overtake me
i do not hear, speak, see or live correctly
i do not know if i will ever be happy again

i am not a person, i am only a lousy number
i am not alive, i breathe and eat and sleep
i am not here to be loved, only cheated and used
i am not significant, and my name is horace

you are a winner, and you will be much more

you are a survivor, and i can see you are honest
you are a fighter, a winner, and quite compassionate
you are worth it, you listen, and help those around you

you are important, i know you and come to you
you succeed, and never let life get you down
you are listening, you counsel and live accordingly
you are on your way to becoming the best you can be

you are valuable, i know your face by heart
you are alive, intimate and full of life and laughter
you are always loved by me, i will die for you
you are significant, and your name is cherished

                                        Toad Lord

                    "i am the king",
                        said he.
                     "i am he",
                        said he.
                  "that is imperishable,
                  that is immeasurable,
                    that is omniscient,
                    that is omnipotent,
                    that is immutable,

                    that is surrealistic,
                    that is unstoppable,
                   that is unmovable."
                        said he.
                     "i am he",
                        said he.
                    "i am the king",
                        said he.
                     "i am he",
                       said he,

"that is the lord"

and Jim leaned over to Melissa and said:
"Man, them frogs sure is loud tonight!"

Spontaneous Psalm #5

Lord I have so much sin in my life…
I don't feel worthy to be called your son…
I don't feel worthy at all Jesus…
But I know you're with me Lord God…
I know you're with me…
I just ask that you take away all these…
Empty feelings inside and I just ask that…
I just ask Lord that you would just…
Heal my heart Lord in here…
It's so cold and calloused…
And broken…
I don't have anything left…
I just feel so empty…
And so dead and so…
Longing for something more and I…
I just want it Lord…
I want more of you…
And I'm just…
I don't have anything to give you…
Just take me away with you God…
And take me away Lord…
I forgive everyone I need to…
I forgive everyone God…
I don't want any darkness in my heart…
Lord come in once again…
I know you want my sin…
I want to begin…
To be with you…
My friend…

Essays

Ruth Ketchum

At the time that I was becoming heavily involved in the art-scene with drew, I also was becoming somewhat involved as friends with Ruth and her kids.

"Kids" was what she called her actors, dancers, singers, and stagehands that made up Heartdance. Ruth herself and her husband Tom are parents of two: Stephanie and Joel. Both have been involved in the play off and on and are a pleasure to know. But Ruth's heart grows beyond her own Physical children into larger heart and grasps the unlovely and misdirected. Her heart was so big that she would embrace the world if physically able. And that's why we loved her. "Mom" to many. "Ruthie" to many more. Ruth was (and is) an inspiration and a joy.

I came on board her crew as a songwriter and found myself saying yes to her when she asked me to play the part of Boo-Dog himself. The former actor had other plans and she was relentless in pursuing my involvement. I was actually shocked to hear myself say yes, but at the time, everything was lining up in a way I had never seen before. Life had never worked this way for me. Seemingly instant friends and family materializing in front of me. Things that were almost impossibility in Indiana became a ready-mix recipe in Oklahoma.

A word on this. I have many friends that I met in Indiana who love me and I love in return. John, Michelle, Laura, Jason, J.B. and Neely. I cannot erase them from my life and would never try to do so. But their friendship was won the hard way and I pray it lasted. Perhaps hundreds of others in many ways I have run into and touched like P.J. or Benji…or Bill, Monty & Chris… but they were in the season and I pray that they are fine. But those you take with you are those you keep. And I am fortunate to have them in my ever-present mind.

But the thing that happened in Oklahoma was entirely new, explosive and lovely.

BANG! Here's your family.

I remember one of the first practices that I came to. Most of it was "Prayer and share", and it was (just so happens) that Amelia had her heart touched in such a way that all of us there were moved to tears because she finally recognized herself as beautiful despite her Bulimia problem. Mind you Amelia was a very beautiful woman and is now married to a very wonderful man named John, but whatever we perceive becomes our reality. And her reality was being "over weight" although she was not.

I believe that we were all crying after this beautiful time with God touching our hearts, and perhaps a whole box of tissue was used to mop our tears, but that is how 'practices' went with the play. God was first, then family, then business. Back words? Perhaps for most business strategy books that you will read, but effectual beyond belief, CHANGED LIVES, CHANGE LIVES.

Having a new script in my hand I drove away from the practice full of conflicting emotions. How are they to get things done with out all of this emotional hoopla going on? Why wasn't everyone present at the practice? Why this, why that. Controversy and turmoil ruled my brain. Until I got used to the idea that they were indeed family and this is how it was. Most of the members of the cast were members of a local church called Tulsa Harvest Church. The abbreviation always cracked me up. T.H.C. I laughed for days when I finally put that together. Not that the pastoral staff condoned the use, but many of the congregation seemed to be former THC users, myself included. As an affiliate of partners in Harvest, the church believed in the ever present guiding of the Holy Spirit, and as growing up in a charismatic background. I have seen many a "Holy-Thing" construed as an action of a bunch of people with THC in their system. All in all, I found Tulsa Harvest to be based in sound New Testament doctrine and quickly become a "member," although this term was jokingly, used by pastors Jim and Richie as someone who shows up. So Ruth I saw not only at practice, but every Sunday as well. Eventually after performing several times as Boo-Dog, I was invited to help with the stage direction and ultimately became the director of the play. Drew became the Executive Director and Ruth, the Playwright. We performed a powerful team and performed at the downtown playhouse as well as churches and prisons. During this episode I became more and more attached to Ruth as I was shown forgiveness, respect, and true love that one shows each other when bonded together for a higher purpose. Still hanging out at the studio, and at this time, working there full time, I was an outsider but soon and indelible part of the jig saw puzzle that was Heartdance. We soon began practice at the church on Tuesday nights. Up until this time that I sold my free time to Ruth's vision, I had begun attending the "Open Mic Night" at the Gypsy Coffeehouse in downtown Tulsa. Attending on and off for six years I was loathe to trade. But I don't regret it. I learned a valuable lesson at Heartdance that could not be learned in a Coffeehouse setting. Issues pertaining to faith mixed up with both, but I was in the right place at the right time. My life changed through the play, thru the relationship with everyone and thru the vision set forth by Ruth. Heartdance was the story of redemption and hope. A story that I desperately needed…

As such a tight knit group of people, we were often forced to deal with personal matters. Like Amelia, we all encountered our demons. There was a time where I was helping Shandale out with a part between Brad, Vince, Noah, and himself. It became personal and a fight arose out of the lines of the play. Noah thought it was a joke but Shandale didn't. Drama, problems, conflict, and thankfully a resolution and forgiveness. I'm glad I was there. I'm glad we all learned more about personal boundaries and about what it means to live thru pain. Later as I told Ruth and Drew about the complication, I learned that communication in all parts was the key to better readability in the bigger picture.

Often, before rehearsal (as we began to call our practices) Ruth and Drew and myself would meet together to talk about what would happen at rehearsal. Personnel issues, complications, and plans were laid out and later, action taken. Actors are a flighty lot and plans were often changed to accommodate. I learned flexibility and apologetics as many times my ideas were shot down in lied of a larger picture challenge.

At first I took this personally. But learned later that sulking child syndrome was for sulking children, and not for adults. I matured with the process in a way I never would have seen anywhere else.

So I became a director, as Drew stepped out of this role and into a larger scope. I filled out our actors with facial expression coaching, upstage challenges and body language. Whenever Ruth came out with a play change I had to bend and fit it in. When Michael came up with choreograph for a fighting scene, I gave it over to him completely. But as Ruth would readily tell you, I tried my utmost and soon began to rely on skills I had learned from Mark Steele who had worked for Tom Newman in Toymakers Dream. Exercise is the key to new muscle. Practice makes more practice. Perfect practice makes perfect. And something that as a concept, I believe was divinely inspired: " Today is a threshold to the cross... Yesterday was our greatest worst performance and tomorrow is our worst best." or something to that affect. Perhaps I was more eloquent when I said it. But I believe people picked up on the jest of the idea. Greatness is never born. it is bred. Potential is only potential until it becomes power and that only comes thru work, work, work.

So I learned what it was to lead, and to follow. With Drew I was learning what it was to create and image on canvas. With Ruth I was learning what it was to create and image on the stage. Each was a design until the canvas was supplied with color. Each artist on stage was the varied color to the play and paint was only as beautiful as its application.

Several months transpired as my relationship grew with Ruth. Around September the pastor of Tulsa Harvest approached her about writing a play for Christmas. She approached me to collaborate and we wrote a beautiful number as we put Heartdance on a side burner for the time. It was during this small season that we had our most arguments and miscommunications. We split the play into two parts and each wrote the bits to be played off of each other. As a crisscross effect, we spliced them together as one comedy (my writing) and one Drama (Ruth's writing). The effect was superb. I invited my family to attend and the audience found themselves stirred by the Drama and laughing the next. The ending scene even had several of us goose-pimpled out with tears in our eyes.

Our second collaboration was to a play that Ruth had written a while ago and she invited me to direct. As an Easter special, I had one of my greatest directing challenges with a middle- aged gentleman named Red. Red was as soft as a Teddy bear and as kind as a kitten. And acting to him became a passion, but he had never acted before in his life. Not knowing my better was to who he was, I prompted to shake him out of his distress on his own abilities. Cornering him in the studio one day I said: "You're a fine actor, you got it in you and don't let anyone tell you differently!" with tears in his eyes he hugged me with a "thank you, you don't know what that means to me." I believe that this small helped him propel to memorize, learn, posture, and project himself to further fill out his part. Red played Satan at the Easter play. He didn't want to do it but he got it down and did an excellent job. I would feel so bad for the consistent coaching, but that's what Ruth led me to be. Consistent. Consistent as God's love, and consistent in leadership.

Working with the group for over two years brought me through many challenges and failures. I had actually just came back from Indiana before I met Ruth and ended up moving back to Indiana on the night of the finale of my career with Heartdance at the last night of the Tulsa Performing Arts Center. It was that night that my Ex-wife, Neely had flown down to take me away from Tulsa for good. She and I had been dancing the love sidestep for so long with breakups and get-togethers and we were both sick of it. She came down to Tulsa to whisk me off my feet for the last time.

paranoia and freedom

ok, so here i sit in the public library thinking about life and liberty and all that is goodness in these united states. i watch movies like "enemy of the state" and get all freaky when i think of how technology can and is being used against us (the citizens thereof). at what small point does my existance pertain to the life of those trapped in the roots of fear? at what conjuncture should i worry about the things that may or not "get me"?

i had an aquaintance named 'brooks' who would come and talk to me when i worked at a certain gas station on the third shift. he would tell me about how he 'knows what they are up to'... and about the secrets of flouride and agent orange. here in this town he has a right to be fearful. the police force uses little monitors to scan cars as they go past every major intersection, and takes the v.i.n. and runs it through their database. the majority of the cops here are paperpushers and record everything that your car does on the street. common knowledge here. it cuts down on the rate of speeders and accidents in the vicinity of those traffice lights where the monitors are.

question: should i worry about them? i used to say when i owned a coffeehouse in indiana: "the police are our friends". i was mainly talking to the drug-pushers and such, but is that really the case or isn't it? i believe that it mostly is. they are there to "serve and protect" the innocent and even the "innocent until proven guilty". sometimes they abuse this power (as is the case for the saying: "power corrupts, and absolute power corrupts absolutly"), often times they do not.

various queries: how is it that i get away with so much of breaking the law and then get all upset when i get pulled over for not using a turn indicator? why don't i just obey in the first place and let there be no more worry? shouldn't i be more concerned with the "law" than that of the guy behind me giving me the finger? hmmm. i suppose i should. perhaps if i did this simple thing, then my paranoia of those "law enforcement officials" around me would grow slimmer, until it vanquished into nothing. but this is not the solution.

my father is good friends with a man who was in the wrong place at the wrong time and is now incarserated for doing something that you or i do every day. the plot is: that he did it with monies not allegated for such a venture. it was bad money and he was busted for doing a favor. he has cause for extreme paranoia. for anger, indeed for resentment. but he chooses not. he chose freedom of the soul, and clarity of mind. why?

his answer was freedom in Christ Jesus. yes, there are satellites that can track our every move, yes some of the things on the x-files are true, yes there are boogy men who work for .gov, but do they concern me? they could but they shouldn't. Christ (when he walked on the earth) gave us a good example for not being unduly upset at government... actually two; now that i think about it.

#1

"give unto ceasers what is ceasers."

paulys translation: "let the force that you recon with be that not of the world in which you live"

you shouldn't be caught up in the movings of black helicoptors, the u.f.o. sightings and the business of the second gunman on the grassy knoll. instead give him (uncle sam) his due, then forget about him. we are protected by our constitution (except for those in the armed forces who are not protected by it, for they are defenders of it, as is the case with my first wife and several friends), and that is a glorious thing. it is not to be taken lightly, and we should be respectful of the ideals in it, if indeed we are citizens of the country in which i speak. give him what he demands and be done with him. exercise your rights, but see them as privilages and not owed favors. we are blessed... don't abuse it. the rest of His quote should sum up what we should be concerned with... "and give unto God, what is Gods."

"if a centurion asks you to go one mile, instead go two."

paulys translation: "go above and beyond what is expected, and let the excess become love."

let's say you have the chance to claim an item on your income taxes and chose to because it will save you money. do it. let the laws work for you but not against you. but do not cheat or skim on anything that is the governments. it will come back on you a hundred times and you will regret it. but let's say the draft comes up. do your part and do it well. if you feel you would be asked to do something not according to your conscience, then go into the chaplain program or communications or even cooking. but do it well, and do it with a smile. point: when you are asked to jump by the u.s.a. ask: "how high, where, and for how long SIR!?!" let be bring to view another scripture from pauls letter to timothy in the new testament: "whatever you do, work at it with all your heart, as working for the Lord and not for man." true love is honoring. plain and simple. honor those in athority over you, and you will be smiled upon divinely.

so,

those over you should not be any concern of yours. secret military spendings... the d.o.d., n.s.a., c.i.a. and various other three letter agencies should not trouble you whatsoever. sure, they may or may not monitor your bank account, they may or not red-flag you for looking up "the turner diaries" or "anarchists cookbook" on the internet... but we should love them, and honor them. i may not have voted for the people in power (side note, my political status is quickly changing from republican to libertarian), but they are there. no fears, no paranoias, no hesitancies. love, serve and honor, and there will be freedom for you.

the ultimate goal of finding freedom from fear is for it to lead you closer to the creator of true life. Jesus Christ loves you, and he made you His. He calls you, and though you may not hear Him on a day to day basis, your life is in His thoughts. need i remind you of the passage in john about love? you know... the famous one? "for God so love the world...'. you know what i'm talking about. so if i (and you) can move together towards life instead of ultimate death (in all of it's many guises) then we can be free, whole and well.

i'll leave you with one of my favorite passages form pauls letter to the galatians: "you all were called to be free! don't use your freedom to indulge in the sinful nature, but rather, serve one another in love!"

thanks for letting me get this off of my chest. lately i have been plagued with "what if this..." or "what if that..." perhaps it all stemmed from watching 'twenty-eight days later' but i think that it was good to talk about it...

To worship a deity

Praise is a weapon. At Jericho, the children of Israel marched and marched and marched and praised. Praise is a great form of expression. Praise can be a wonderful tool. Praise can be many, many things. Praise, in the dictionary, is a way of expressing high acclimation to a person or persons that you would not normally give to any other person. But praise to me is just a way of telling the people around me, the angels, the demons, and almighty God himself just how much I love Him.

If I had lived in the days when Christ had walked the earth, I would have liked to have asked him all about praise and worship. You see, today, we have narrowed it down to a slick formula. Three fast songs, two slow songs, hymn number one sixty four, the choirs special, the statement of faith, then the mourning (oops, I mean morning) announcements, and then pastor comes up. Barf! That's not the way to reverence God in a proper attitude of humbleness, gratefulness, and loving-kindness! That is hypocrisy! They say that whatever you do most in a day is what you're most committed to. Well, just how many hours a day do you spend sleeping? How about eating? How long do you spend in your car; driving, listening to that new talk show, and honking at the jerk in front of you? Count all of those times, and then count your hours of prayer, scripture reading, meditation, worship, memorization, and proclamation. Hmmm. . . I wonder which list has more hours written down? Just how much do we worship and praise Him?

I wish we could know God as Jesus prayed in John chapter seventeen. I wish I could know Him like that. How I long to be able to reach out to Him and to be close to Him, and for Him to just sit awhile with me. For Him to just hold me. Moment by moment, till forever passes by. But I'm still earth-tied. I just wish we could see Him for how He really is. If only for one nano-second! I wonder if you would die? Who cares! I'll be forever with Him anyway!

People, come on. Let's get with the program. To really worship The Father implies that we crawl up on His lap and kiss his cheek. When was the last time you heard such intimacy preached from a religious pulpit? It's easier to live that one out in the real world, like Jesus did. With the prostitutes, the refugees, the drug-dealers, the sick and the dying.

Jesus called The Father "Abba" which is the most simplistic form of fatherhood ever spoken. Translated it is da-da. I call him Daddy sometimes. It feels really weird. So many of us have a warped view of what a Father should be. I try to worship him as he ought to be. I try to praise Him as he deserves to be. Nothing I do will ever come close to the awesomeness he possess in him little finger. Try to give Him the honor He commands. Try to praise Him, and try your hardest to worship the King. The tremendous truth is... You can!

Ye Olde Coffee Shoppe

So such is life, I met a girl and we got married. I had the presence of spirit to have saved my virginity for her, and around the time that my mother passed away, I was twenty five and ready to settle down. Life was suddenly wonderful. Sex was new and marriage was good. We started a Bible study in our home and went to a local church in my new home in rural Indiana. We were so on fire for Jesus, we started a 'zine and discussed Christian Music Bands, Theology and life as Generation X'ers. Things were good and I took a Youth Pastor job in neighboring Fort Wayne. That went well until the Pastor fired me for being too much like Jesus (no joke), and then we opened a coffeeshop.

The New Planet Cafe. Yeah, yeah, yeah...I know what you're thinking. The title of this book talks about the earth being a flat, motionless plane and I named my coffeeshop after a planet. Pretty hypocritical. Sure, there was that. But there was also the fact that no one wanted to hear about my views on an earth that the Bible said was fixed on pillars. I was compromising with my new bride and that was that. It still was pretty bold though to have a "Christian Coffeeshop" in a heathen land. My wife and I had tinkered around with band promotion around the city and we had youth pastors from a Lutheran and Presbyterian church at by our side but the little church I worked at wouldn't have any inter-church cooperation and so we used the coffeeshop to do all the work. We started another 'zine and soon we were pretty busy selling coffee and peddling Jesus.

The name of the place came from Revelation 21, where the promise is that we will all have a new heaven and a new earth one day. That the shape of the earth was a question was still a little out there for most people... I mean, I wanted to believe in the Bible's viewpoint, but no one agreed with me, so I kept my mouth shut. You think it's hard to be a flat earth believer today? It was pretty scary back in '97 to be a flat earther. No one wanted to hear it. Besides, there was a lot of cool stuff that I could be involved in to take my time away from the discipline of thinking about the shape of the earth so I let it go.

I had articles to write and pages to design for the magazine and ads to sell and coffee to buy and we had just bought a new house and just gotten a dog and I had a car given to me and things were going great! We had a summer music festival and we had twenty bands come and we had rented out the park and there was just a ton of kids there and it was awesome and it really looked like God was bringing revival to the unchurched and unwanted people of Fort Wayne. God was moving.

And then the Vineyard asked me not to come back. And then the police came and arrested some people at the coffeeshop. And then the Landlord raised my rent. And then my wife told me that her boyfriend had gotten her pregnant.